G.G. & Edward,

Adventure Awaits!

Ben Gibson

Pirate Treasure

TRAVELING TRUNK ADVENTURE 1

By **BENJAMIN FLINDERS**

Illustrations By NICOLAUS SERR

FLINDERS PRESS

www.flinderspress.com

For my sons, who make each day an adventure

Traveling Trunk Adventure #1: Pirate Treasure

Library of Congress Control Number: 2010924528
ISBN: 978-0-9843955-4-5

Printed in China

Contents

Chapter 1
Jungle Room

Slivers of spring sunlight stole through the cracks in the leaf-shaped window blinds. Unable to ignore the shaft of light on his face, Ethan sat up, stretched, and rubbed his blue eyes.

Crawling to the edge of the top bunk, he grabbed the green rope hanging from the vaulted ceiling and, in Tarzan fashion, swung down.

Thump!

He tried to do a flip, but instead landed on his back in the middle of a giant, blue LoveSac beanbag strategically placed on the floor.

The bunk beds looked like branches growing from a massive tree planted in the bedroom Ethan shared with his eight-year-old brother Dallin. Three years older, Ethan got the top bunk, which meant he had the pleasure of swinging out of the tree bed each morning. That was the best part about waking up, though he still couldn't do a flip like Dallin.

Climbing off the bag, Ethan noticed his younger brother still sleeping, his brown hair a mess, and drool dribbling down his cheek. "Dallin, wake up. It's Saturday! Dad will be home from his business trip today."

At the mention of Dad, Dallin's green eyes popped open and he sat up, wiping his cheek. "Dad's home?"

"No, but Mom said he should be back this morning," Ethan said. "Hurry, I smell cinnamon rolls. Breakfast must be ready."

Tumbling down the stairs, Ethan and Dallin raced each other to the kitchen.

"Dad!" Dallin exclaimed, surprised to see his father standing at the table. He rushed past Ethan and into the dining room, giving his father a ferocious bear hug, complete with growl. He would have jumped into his arms, but they were already holding his three-year-old sister, Kaitlyn.

"You're early," Ethan smiled as Dad ruffled his blond hair.

"No, you two are late," said Dad. "It's after 8:30! You slept in this morning."

Looking at the old grandfather clock in the dining room, Dallin saw that the little hand was between the VIII and the IX, and the big hand pointed at the VII.

"Eight thirty-five," Dallin read aloud, proud to have recently learned his Roman numerals. Then he checked his digital wristwatch just to make sure. "So what did you bring us?"

"Eat your breakfast first boys," Mom said, placing two bowls of cinnamon-raisin oatmeal on the table.

"Aw, oatmeal," Ethan complained. "I thought we were having cinnamon rolls."

"Eat up, boys, then come up to your bedroom and I'll show you the surprise I got for you," Dad said, putting Kaitlyn into her highchair.

"Cool," the boys said together, their eyes twinkling as they sat down to eat.

Chapter 2
Treasure Chest

"On your mark, get set, go!" Ethan counted down, and together he and Dallin charged up the stairs. "First one to the top wins."

As they neared the last step, Ethan was in the lead.

In desperation, Dallin dove over the last two steps and onto his belly. The bowl of oatmeal sloshed around, threatening to come back up.

"I win!" Dallin cheered, letting fly a loud burp.

"Lucky dive," Ethan said begrudgingly, helping his younger brother up. "I hope you barf on whatever Dad got you."

"It'll never happen. I have an iron stomach." Dallin punched himself in the gut to prove his point.

With Dallin leading the way, they headed for their bedroom.

Living in a condominium complex in Los Angeles did not give the brothers much open space to play. To compensate for the lack of a backyard, their parents designed their bedroom to look like a jungle. The tree-shaped bunk beds, banana-leaf blinds, and the vine rope hanging from the ceiling helped keep their imaginations alive. Every time their dad went on a business trip, he brought them a souvenir that would add to the atmosphere of their private jungle. This time was going to be different.

Dallin was the first to see their dad taking everything out of their old toy box and putting the contents into a much larger chest. If he had kept with tradition, the chest should have looked like an old tree stump, or at least have animal-print fabric on the outside to fit in with the jungle room. It was neither of these. The beat-up old trunk made as much sense in their bedroom as a porcupine in a ball pit.

"What's this?" Ethan asked.

"Aarrgh, me laddies. This here be the cursed treasure chest of Cap'n Bartelmy, the terror of the Seven Seas," Dad said in his best pirate voice.

He pulled out a black sheet, flapped it in the air and then draped it over the chest. It had two white swords crossed below a large skull.

"Cool, is that a real pirate flag?" asked Dallin. He didn't care if the new toy box didn't fit the décor of the rest of the room; if it was a real pirate treasure chest, then that was all right with him.

"This here be the Jolly Roger," Dad said.

"The what?"

Switching back to his normal voice, he continued, "The Jolly Roger is what pirates called their flag."

"Where did you get it?" said Dallin.

"I found this stuff at a flea market. The old woman I bought it from said they once belonged to her son-in-law, a pirate from the 1600's. She mentioned something about trying to get this trunk into the 'right hands' for the past several hundred of years."

"Right hands for what?" asked Ethan.

"I have no idea," Dad said. "She was a mysterious woman. You would have loved her, Ethan. She looked like a witch from one of your books; old and wrinkly, with a hairy, black mole on her chin."

"Wow, she must be like a million years old," Dallin said.

"No, that would have made her like three or four hundred years old," Ethan corrected. "Besides, there's no way she could be that old."

"Yu-huh. If she was a witch, she could be."

"There's no such thing as witches."

Dad laughed. "Yes, obviously, she was joking. She couldn't have been that old. But she did tell me that the original owner's name was Captain Bartelmy. History remembers him as Cap'n Black Bart, the terror of the Seven Seas. Before becoming a pirate, the captain was a successful merchant in the New World. Then one day he up and left his wife and kids and took to the sea, converting his crew to piracy. They robbed and plundered throughout the Caribbean, and were as nasty as pirates could be."

"So why did you get us an old pirate chest?" Ethan asked. "It doesn't exactly fit in with our bedroom." He had been hoping for a rope ladder to climb up his bunk bed.

"When I told the lady I wanted to buy a gift for my eight and eleven-year-old boys, she insisted I get you this trunk." Their dad paused, shook his head as if he had forgotten something, and rubbed his scruffy chin. "Funny thing is, I didn't want to buy the trunk, and I still can't figure out why I did. Now that I think about it, I don't even remember paying for it."

They all stared at the beat-up, old trunk for a minute.

Dallin finally broke the silence. "Did you check inside for any pirate gold, or perhaps an old treasure map?"

Yawning, Dad turned and headed for the door. "Not yet. You can do the honors. I've been up all night on an airplane. I need a nap. When I wake up, we can go to the lumber store and find a flag pole to hoist the Jolly Roger above your new chest."

"Thanks, Dad," Dallin said.

"Yeah, thanks," Ethan echoed. "We're glad you're back."

Chapter 3
Pirate Clothes

Removing the Jolly Roger, the brothers examined their new toy box. Ethan ran his fingers over the thick planks of wood, dented and scarred by decades of travel to who-knew-where. There were several gaps between the boards, like an old man's rotting smile. The only thing that kept the trunk together were strips of weathered metal fastened to the edges and across the top. Once upon a time there had been a latch and lock, but they were long gone, the sharp edges worn smooth by the passing of time.

Dallin doubted any treasure would still be in the trunk, but that didn't damper his excitement. "Want to play pirates?"

Ethan quickly lost interest. "I think I'll do some reading." Being a sixth grader, he was more interested in reading about adventures than pretending to go on them. He grabbed one of his favorite books, *Peter Pan*, and headed for the big beanbag.

Dallin did enough reading in school. Saturdays were meant for playing. Opening the dome-shaped lid, he was surprised by the strong, salty ocean smell that wafted out of the chest. For a brief moment, he thought he could hear the crashing of waves and the cawing of seagulls.

"Hey!" he blurted out. "What happened to our toys? They've disappeared!"

"Ha, ha," Ethan said sarcastically, looking over the top of his dog-eared book. "Like I'm going to fall for that. You just want me to come over there and play with you."

"No, really. The trunk is empty," Dallin said, tilting the chest so Ethan could see inside. The chest was indeed empty, except for a pile of dirty old rags lying in the bottom. "Dad must have taken them out with our old box."

Ethan nudged his book into folds of the beanbag so he wouldn't lose his place. "No, I saw him put our stuff in there." He got up for a closer look. "Maybe there is a trap door or something."

"Yeah, like a secret compartment where the pirates kept their treasure maps," Dallin said enthusiastically.

After knocking, hitting, kicking and pulling failed to reveal any hidden compartments, Dallin headed for the bedroom door. "Oh well, it was worth a try. I'll go ask Dad what he did with our toys."

"Wait; he just laid down. We better let him get some rest."

"Ah, okay," Dallin sighed, slumping onto the beanbag. It was going to be a very dull Saturday morning.

"Fine, I guess we can play pirates for a little bit," Ethan said. He reached into the trunk and pulled out what Dallin had thought were just a bunch of rags. "Dad must have got us these pirate costumes to go along with the chest."

"Awesome!"

Ethan sorted out two long-sleeved shirts complete with worn-out leather vests, two pairs of knee-length pants, belts, bandanas to tie around their heads, and even two pairs of used shoes that fit them perfectly.

After getting dressed, Ethan said, "These are cabin-boy clothes. Too bad Dad didn't get us captain costumes."

"What would a captain look like?"

"You know—the captain wears one of those big three-pointed hats, and he would have a sword or two, plus a pistol."

"A sword would have been cool."

"Yeah," Ethan agreed.

Looking into the chest to make sure it was empty, Ethan saw two gold-handled daggers.

"Hey, check these out!" he said, holding up the knives for Dallin to look at. "How come we didn't see these before?"

Red rubies and green emeralds adorned the gold handles, and a fancy "B" was engraved on the end.

"Cool knives," Dallin said, taking one from Ethan and pulling the blade from the black leather sheath. "This is a lot sharper than your Boy Scout pocketknife."

Leather loops on the sheath allowed the boys to hang the daggers from their belts. The same fancy "B" was branded on the leather.

"That's better," Ethan said, putting the dagger on his belt. "These are definitely a lot cooler than a rope ladder. How do I look?"

Before Dallin could answer, there was a soft knock on their bedroom door.

"E-hen, Da-win, ah you in heah?" their sister called out from behind the closed door.

Both boys looked at each other.

"Quick, hide inside the chest," Ethan said. "If Kaitlyn sees our daggers, she'll want one too, and then Mom will find out. She'll put them with the camping gear, and we won't get to play with them again 'til summertime."

They jumped into the chest, barely able to squeeze inside, and managed to get the lid closed just as their bedroom door began to swing open.

They waited quietly, listening for their little sister to leave.

"Wouldn't it be cool if this was a real pirate treasure chest, and when we climbed out we became pirates," Dallin whispered.

As soon as Dallin said this, the trunk shifted, as if someone had bumped it.

"Whoa! What was that?" Dallin said.

"Shh, I hear something," Ethan whispered.

"Hear what?"

"It sounds like the beach."

Pressing his ear against the inside of the chest, Dallin listened.

"You're right, it sounds like seagulls," he said. "Wait, I think I hear singing, too."

Slowly they raised the lid and peeked out. They couldn't believe what they saw.

"Uh, Dallin, I don't think we're in Los Angeles anymore."

Climbing out of the trunk, the brothers stood in a stately room with wood-paneled walls, ceiling and floor. A four-poster bed, hand-carved cabinets, and an ornate desk and chairs adorned the room. Brass lanterns were mounted to the walls and a gently-swaying candle chandelier hung above a round table revealing a dirty map with a large black X on it.

Dancing sunlight filtered through a long set of small windows set into the wall behind the table. From the windows the boys could see dark-blue foamy ocean rolling behind the ship, with miniature green mountains floating in the distance.

"We're on a ship in the middle of the ocean," Dallin gasped, breathing in the salty air.

As if to eliminate any doubt of where they were, the floor pitched and rolled beneath their feet, slamming the chest closed. Ethan grabbed onto Dallin to avoid toppling over.

They could still hear the seagulls, but the cawing was growing weaker while the singing was getting louder.

"What's going on, Dallin?" Ethan said, his head spinning as he tried to make sense of their new surroundings.

"I don't know. Let's find out!"

Staggering to a large wooden door, Dallin's progress was halted by Ethan's hand on his shoulder. "Wait, don't you think this is a little weird? Maybe we should climb back into the trunk and see if it will take us home before we get into any trouble."

"But…" Dallin hesitated, looking back and forth from the trunk to the door. Dallin's fingers itched to reach out and open the door and reveal the mystery hiding behind it.

"If the trunk takes us home, we'll come right back, okay?" Ethan tried to sound convincing.

"But…what if the magic stops working?"

"Better stuck at home than here," Ethan said. "Besides, we don't even know where here is."

Dallin looked longingly at the door. "Oh, all right."

Ethan sighed with relief, let go of his brother, and turned back to the trunk.

"Just one quick peek first," Dallin said, lunging for the door.

"No, wait!" Ethan yelled, springing after Dallin. But the ship abruptly rose and fell, sending the boys crashing to the floor.

As Dallin fell, he grabbed the door handle for support, and accidentally yanked it down. A brisk gust of wind pushed the door open, ushering into the room the smell of fish and the harmonious sound of men singing in unison.

Both boys froze. From his position on the floor, Ethan saw a ragtag crew of sailors swabbing the deck, pulling on ropes, and moving around a large Spanish galleon ship, singing as they worked:

We sail across the ocean blue,
From anywhere to Timbuktu,
A bloodthirsty captain and crew,
Until we find what we are due.

Give a heave, ho, hi, ho, sweat on the deck.
Give a heave, ho, hi, ho, or hang from yer neck.

Blue sky above, and ocean below,
We pillage and plunder as we go,
Filling our chests 'til they overflow,
We've yet to strike rich, so on we go.

Give a heave, ho, hi, ho, sweat on the deck.
Give a heave, ho, hi, ho, or hang from yer neck.

Some men fight 'cause they're noble and bold,
Some men fight just to do as they're told,
But pirates fight for treasure and gold,
All day and night 'til our hearts grow cold.

Give a heave, ho, hi, ho, sweat on the deck.
Give a heave, ho, hi, ho, or hang from yer neck.

As the chantey continued, Ethan and Dallin stared at each other in shock.

"Is this a real pirate ship?" Dallin asked, his eyes bulging with excitement.

Ethan climbed to his feet and joined Dallin at the door, watching the singing men move about the deck. A burly pirate with an untidy brown beard pulled on a thick rope, hoisting a billowing black flag. He sang as he pulled, until the flag reached the top of the mast and snapped to attention in the wind, revealing a large skull with two white swords crossed underneath: the Jolly Roger.

"No way!" Dallin cried out. "This is a real pirate ship!"

Hearing Dallin's exclamation, the brown-bearded pirate looked up and stared straight into his eyes.

"Intruders!" he shouted, pulling a sword from his side and pointing it at the boys.

"Quick, back to the treasure chest!" Ethan yelled, pulling Dallin away from the door and slamming it shut.

They were half-way across the room when the ship rocked to the side, sending the boys crashing against the four-poster bed and onto the floor. They jumped up and lunged for the chest as pirates charged into the room.

Ethan threw open the lid and was about to jump inside, but there wasn't any room. The chest was full of treasure.

Stunned, and unable to move, several strong pirates grabbed them by the arms and yanked them away from the treasure chest.

Ethan and Dallin stared into the scowling face of the brown-bearded pirate.

"Stowaways," he growled. "Take 'em to the cap'n."

"I think we're in trouble now," Ethan mumbled.

"Please tell me I'm dreaming, please tell me I'm dreaming, please tell me I'm dreaming," Dallin chanted, his eyes closed as the pirates dragged them away.

Chapter 4
Captain Black Bart

Looking up, Ethan and Dallin saw the quarter deck and helm—the back part of the ship. The captain stood behind a large wheel, steering the ship through the ocean.

Dallin knew he was the captain from what Ethan had told him earlier. He wore a big, three-pointed hat, a short sword known as a cutlass strapped to one side, and several pistols protruded from underneath his long black overcoat.

"Stowaways, Cap'n Bartelmy, err, I mean, Cap'n Black Bart," the brown-bearded pirate reported. "Found 'em in yer quarters, sir, tryin' to get into the treasure chest. They had these strapped to their belts."

The pirate held out two gold-handled daggers, showing them to the captain and assembled crew. Several menacing "Aarrghs" issued from the crew.

The ship rolled again, and the boys teetered into one of their captors.

"Landlubbers! They ain't even got their sea legs," one of the pirates chuckled as both boys continued to sway.

"Thank you, Bosun. Lieutenant Howl, take the helm," the captain ordered, walking away from the wooden wheel.

"Squawk! Aye, aye, Cap'n," a colorful red, green and blue parrot squawked from the lieutenant's shoulder as he took over at the helm.

The captain glared at Ethan and Dallin as he stood in front of them. "I be Captain Black Bart, soon to be the most feared pirate of the Seven Seas. And who be ye?"

Captain Black Bart had long hair that slithered from beneath his hat like poisonous eels, a weathered face, and a white scar that ran across his right eye and down his dirty cheek.

"I—I am Ethan, and th—th—this is my brother Dallin," Ethan stuttered, his knees knocking together faster than his racing heart.

"How did ye get on me ship?" the captain demanded, squinting at them.

"We climbed out of your magic treasure chest," Dallin blurted.

"Magicians?" the captain said in surprise, taking a step backward. "And ye were tryin' to get into me treasure chest, eh? That means ye be thieves as well."

"No," Ethan protested. "We were not trying to steal…"

"Not trying to steal!" Captain Black Bart yelled.

"Then why did ye have these?" he demanded, taking the daggers from the bosun and holding them out for the boys to look at.

"We got them…from…our chest," Ethan stammered.

"Ye mean from *MY* chest!" the captain bellowed.

He turned his back on the boys and began pacing the deck.

"Landlubbers and thieves," the captain yelled, loud enough for his entire crew to hear. "What do we be doin' with landlubbers and thieves?"

No one answered.

Ethan and Dallin glanced at the crew, who were looking at each other with confused expressions. The crew wasn't sure how to answer.

"Landlubbers and thieves!" the captain cried out, louder this time. "What do *PIRATES* do with landlubbers and thieves?"

He added extra emphasis on "pirates" as if to remind his crew what they were.

"Do we drop 'em off at shore, Cap'n?" a brawny, bald pirate asked timidly.

"Nay," the captain bellowed. "Pirates don't be droppin' prisoners off at shore, Mr. Stiles."

"Uh, Cap'n, I changed me name to Lance Killjoy," the pirate said, his eye twitching nervously.

"Now why did ye do that Mr. Stiles, or Mr. Killjoy, whichever ye be?" the captain demanded.

"Ye said to, sir," Mr. Killjoy answered. "This mornin' ye told us all to be gettin' pirate-sounding names, the kind which strike fear into the hearts of men."

The captain paused, thinking.

"Right ye be, Mr. Killjoy. That there be a great name by the way," the captain complimented, patting the burly pirate on his thick shoulders. "But somebody best let me know what ye all be calling yerselves now."

Dallin leaned over to Ethan and said, "I don't think they've been pirates for very long."

Overhearing the boy's comment, Captain Black Bart stopped pacing and scowled.

"Ye be right," he said bending down to Dallin's level, his good eye bulging. "We ain't been pirates fer very long, but we be learnin' quickly."

Mumbling to himself, the captain stood up and announced, "No, me hearties, *pirates* do not release thieves. *Pirates* make thieves walk the plank!"

"Wha—what do you mean, walk the plank?" Ethan stuttered. "You mean, like into the ocean?"

"Aye," the captain growled. "It be a short trip to Davy Jones' locker."

"Cap'n," a short pirate with a high-pitched voice interrupted. "We don't have a plank!"

Ethan and Dallin sighed with relief.

Captain Black Bart thought for a moment, and then addressed the midget pirate, "Mr. Cuddle...ye still be Mr. Cuddle, right?"

"No, sir," he squeaked, trying to stand as tall as he could. "I changed me name to Darren Deeds, sir."

"Right then, Mr. Deeds it is. How are we ever going to become feared pirates if we don't even have a plank? This won't do, this just won't do. Mateys, throw these young scallywags in the brig 'til we make ourselves a plank."

"Aarrgh," the crew complied, dragging Ethan and Dallin down into the belly of the ship.

Chapter 5
Fish Breath Cooky

The metal prison door clanged shut, with Ethan and Dallin trapped behind it.

"Now don't ye be goin' nowhere. Har, har, har," the bosun laughed. The pirates walked back up the stairs, taking the lantern with them.

As they retreated, it got darker and darker in the brig.

"Ethan is this real, or are we dreaming?"

"I don't know, Dallin. It sure feels real," Ethan said, trying to keep his fear under control.

"It sure smells real, too," Dallin said, pinching his nose to keep the stench out.

As their eyes adjusted to the darkness, shapes began to take form. Large barrels, crates, caskets, and other supplies were stacked up or tied in bundles. Without a lantern, the only light in this part of the ship came from cracks in the ceiling, which also happened to be the floor of the deck above.

For several minutes they stood at the prison door looking up the stairs, swaying as the ship teetered from side to side.

They could hear men moving about and working above them. Some had begun singing again, a new song about swashbuckling and keelhauling. They could also hear the creaking of the ship as it rode through the ocean.

"This would be so cool if we weren't about to walk the plank," Dallin said.

"Yeah, I guess so."

After swaying for a few more minutes Dallin asked, "How did we get here anyway?"

Thinking hard, Ethan guessed, "The trunk Dad gave us must be magic, and somehow opened a doorway to the original chest. If we can get back inside the treasure chest, I think it will take us home."

Dallin looked as confused as Ethan felt.

"But it was full of treasure," Dallin said. "It was empty when we climbed out of it. How is it supposed to work with all that treasure in it?"

"I've read about stuff like this in books before, but never thought it could really happen," Ethan said. "Maybe we have to do something first, before we can go home."

"Like what?"

"I don't know. The chest belonged to Captain Bartelmy; maybe we need to help him somehow."

"Help that meany?" Dallin scowled angrily, balling his hands into fists. "No way! He is going to make us walk the plank, remember?"

"He weren't always a meany," a froggy voice croaked from the gloom behind them.

Dallin and Ethan jumped so far they smacked into the metal door.

Turning around, Ethan stuttered, "Wh—who's there?"

Sitting in the shadows of the prison was a man, all skin-and-bones, leaning against the curved wall of the wooden ship. He reached for the bars to pull himself up, but instead of a left hand, the boys saw a sharp hook. Both boys gasped.

"Ye can call me Fish-Breath Cooky. I'm the cook on this here ship," the pirate grunted, rattling the bars as he struggled to unhook his claw.

"Aarrgh, blasted hook!" he cursed, finally pulling it free. "But since Cap'n be turnin' us all into pirates, I guess I'll change me name to Meany Cooky. 'Tis better than Fish-Breath Cooky."

"How about Tough Cookie," Dallin suggested, his fear dwindling. "Then people will think you are dangerous and strong."

"Oh, 'tis much better; t'anks for the idea, lad." He flashed a big smile at the boys, proud of his new name. With their eyes adjusted to the dark, they could see several of his teeth were missing. He had a long, curved nose, big ears, and clumps of curly hair on the side of his head. With his crooked grin, Tough Cooky did not look like he would live up to his name, despite the sharp hook.

"You're awful skinny to be a cook," Dallin observed.

Using his metal hook as a toothpick, he said, "That's 'cause I don't like me cookin'."

"And you're a prisoner too?" Ethan asked.

"Aye, lad," he nodded. "The cap'n caught me writin' a letter to me wife, so he threw me in the brig."

"See Ethan, I told you the captain is mean. He won't even let his crew write letters to their family."

Tough Cooky looked around the brig to make sure
they were alone, then lowering his voice said, "Truth
be, I was tellin' me wife that we was all turnin' pirates,
and for her not to be worryin' about me. Ye see, Cap'n

threw me in the brig 'cause we weren't supposed to be tellin' no one, savvy?"

"Oh, I see. So you are, like, in a time-out," Dallin said with understanding. "Yeah, I get sent to my room when I disobey, too."

"But at least Mom doesn't forget about us, Dallin. It looks like the captain forgot about you, Mr. Cooky. You must have been down here for weeks," Ethan said, looking Tough Cooky over.

The pirate was dirty, stinky, and his breath smelled like rotten fish. No wonder the crew called him Fish-Breath Cooky.

"What? Naw, just got thrown in here last night," Tough Cooky said, waving his hook in dismissal. "We only left port this mornin'. I ain't even been a pirate a whole day yet."

That triggered something in Ethan's memory.

"Dallin, remember what Dad told us about Captain Bartelmy?" Ethan asked, turning to his brother in the dim light. "He said the captain had been a successful merchant, but then one day he left his wife and kids and became a pirate."

"Oh, yeah."

"What's that?" Tough Cooky asked. He removed a ball of wax from his ear then flicked it onto the grimy floor. "I think ye got it wrong there, laddie. T'was the other way 'round. Mrs. Bartelmy took the kids and left the cap'n; and from what me ears be hearin', the missus called him some nasty names."

"Good for her," Dallin said. "I'm going to call him some nasty names too if he tries to make us walk the plank!"

"Well hold on there, young buccaneer," Tough Cooky said. "The cap'n weren't never mean. At least not 'til last night when he rounded us all up and said we was leavin' to become pirates. Before that, the cap'n had always been nice and fair to everybody, that's why we all be stickin' with the cap'n, even though he decided to turn pirate. None of us could figure why the missus left him. All our wives be jealous of Mrs. Bartelmy 'cause the cap'n be so generous and treatin' her so well."

"That just doesn't make sense," Ethan said. "Why would she leave him if he was so nice to her?"

"Women be mysterious creatures, lad," the cook said thoughtfully.

"Hmm," Ethan sighed, sitting down to think.

"I want to know what the captain's wife called him," Dallin said, smiling deviously.

Glancing up the stairs to make sure they were empty, Tough Cooky whispered, "She left a note at the cap'n's house callin' him a 'Stingy Sour Crust,' and took the kids and ran off to her mother's house."

Settling back down into his corner, Tough Cooky added, "Yup, we had just unloaded from a successful voyage last night. Several of us helped take the cap'n's treasure chest and other goods up to his lodgings. I was standin' there when the cap'n walked into an empty house and found the wife's note sittin' on the table. After readin' the note, the cap'n marched us all back to the ship, and we been pirates ever since. He was so angry that we set sail as soon as we re-supplied. Didn't even get a chance to see our wives again—that's why I was writin' the letter that got me thrown into the brig."

Ethan could tell there was something wrong with this story. He did not doubt Tough Cooky, but something seemed a little fishy, besides the pirate's breath.

If only I could see the note, maybe I could figure out a way to save ourselves and help Captain Black Bart, Ethan thought.

His thinking was interrupted by the sound of footsteps tromping down the wooden stairs.

The brown-bearded pirate and two other men approached the prison.

Ethan and Dallin backed away from the door.

"Get up, Fish-Breath Cooky!" the bosun ordered, unlocking the door. "Cap'n wants lunch soon, and he be in a foul temper, so ye best make one of his favorite dishes."

"If I'm goin' to be a pirate, me new name be Tough Cooky, not Fish-Breath Cooky no more," Tough Cooky croaked, shuffling out of the brig.

He stopped, and turning to the bosun asked, "What about the lads? I could be usin' their help in the galley."

A cruel smirk formed beneath the scruffy, brown beard. "These two have a rendezvous with Davy Jones' locker."

"What is Davy Jones' locker, anyway?" Dallin asked confused.

"Har, har, har," the bosun laughed. "Davy Jones' locker be the bottom of the sea, which is where ye be headin'. Grab 'em, men!"

Chapter 6
The Plank

Blue waves rolled lazily across the peaceful ocean, lifting and lowering the pirate ship in a rhythmic pattern. Cauliflower clouds danced across the blue sky while a gentle breeze kissed the sails.

What a great day to go for a swim, Dallin thought, as his captors led him and his brother to the side of the ship. *Oh cool, a diving board.*

A long piece of flat timber was rigged to the side of the ship, sticking out six feet into the empty air.

"Put 'em on the plank," the bosun growled.

Dallin shivered when he realized the diving board was in fact the dreaded plank.

The pirates did as they were told. The boys were too shocked to fight back as their hands were tied to one another.

The crew quickly gathered on the main deck, excited to take part in their first plank walk as pirates.

The captain stood stoically at the helm, steering into the blue horizon. When he saw his two prisoners swaying on the plank, he turned the wheel over to Lieutenant Howl and his parrot.

"Have you figured out how to save us yet?" Dallin asked, terrified as he watched Captain Black Bart approach, sword in hand.

"Maybe when we hit the water we'll wake up in our beds," Ethan said, squeezing his brother's hand.

"I sure hope so. And if not?"

"Swim for the shore, I guess," Ethan shrugged, glancing over his shoulder at the cold water below.

They could still see the coast bobbing in the distance, but since the pirates had tied Dallin's right hand to Ethan's left, swimming would be impossible.

Captain Black Bart stopped in front of Ethan and Dallin, and then turned his back on them, facing his crew. "Me hearties, we be brothers in piracy now. We take what we want, and give nuttin' back. But those who take from his brother, the plank is what they be gettin'. Do we have an accord?"

"Aye, Cap'n," they all bellowed.

"What's an accord?" Dallin whispered to Ethan.

"I think it means, 'does everyone agree'."

Removing his hat and placing it over his cold heart, Captain Black Bart pointed at the boys with his sword, and pronounced judgment, "Then as cap'n of this here vessel, I declare these two scallywags guilty of theft, by their own admission, and sentence them to walk the plank."

Stepping up to the boys he frowned, his scarred face only a few feet away. "Give me regards to Davy Jones."

"Never, you meany!" Dallin spat.

Lunging at the captain, Dallin raised his balled fist and swung as hard as he could at the captain's big nose. But the captain was too quick. He caught Dallin's arm firmly by the wrist, growled, and then squeezed hard.

BEEP—BEEP—BEEP

"Aarrgh," the captain yelled, dropping Dallin's arm and leaping backward.

He stared at Dallin in amazement.

In the shadow of the main sail Dallin's wristwatch flashed bright blue.

BEEP—BEEP—BEEP

As the wristwatch beeped and flashed again, Captain Black Bart backed away from the boys, fear in his eyes.

BEEP—BEEP—BEEP

"Dallin, your watch alarm," Ethan whispered. "Hold out your wrist and walk toward them."

BEEP—BEEP—BEEP

The brothers jumped off the plank together, Dallin waving his flashing wrist menacingly at the pirates.

BEEP—BEEP—BEEP

Wherever he turned his arm, the pirates gave out a howl of fear and shrank back.

BEEP—BEEP—BEEP

"Blimey! Make it stop, Magician!" the captain cried.

BEEP—BEEP—BEEP

"Only if you promise to free us," Ethan yelled.

BEEP—BEEP—BEEP

"Parlay, parlay!" the captain begged.

BEEP—BEEP—BEEP

"What does parlay mean?" Dallin asked, swinging his arm at the bosun.

BEEP—BEEP—BEEP

"It means the cap'n wants to negotiate with ye," the bosun said in fear.

The beeping stopped and the flashing light ceased.

"Why did you stop it?" Ethan whispered.

Dallin whispered back, "It stops automatically after one minute."

"Thank ye," the captain cried, falling to his knees. "Oh powerful magicians, don't be bringin' yer wrath upon us humble sailors."

"Spare us," the bosun whimpered.

"We won't harm you," Ethan yelled out. "But only if you agree to take us back to shore and set us free."

"Do we have an accord?" Dallin yelled.

"Aye, aye," the pirates bellowed in unison.

Dallin smiled triumphantly.

Chapter 7
Polly Wanna Cracker

Captain Black Bart scurried back to the helm like a chastised puppy dog with its tail between its legs. He turned the ship around and headed back to port. They wouldn't make landfall until night, so he sent Lieutenant Howl to deal with Ethan and Dallin.

"What do we do now?" Dallin asked.

"First thing we do is find someone to cut these ropes off our arms," Ethan said, looking around.

The crew had already scattered, finding chores or other odd jobs to occupy themselves. None had stuck around, though they could see several pirates peeking around corners, or glancing at them while pretending to do something else.

Lieutenant Howl approached cautiously, his colorful parrot pacing back and forth across his shoulders as if it owned the deck.

"Squawk! Ahoy there mateys," the bird greeted in a high-pitched voice.

"Cool, a talking parrot!" Dallin said. "Polly wanna cracker?"

The lieutenant, and the parrot, ignored Dallin.

"Hello, Lieutenant," Ethan said. "Can you cut off these ropes?"

The boys held up their bound hands.

"Fiddle-de-dee, I'll cut ye free," the parrot said as Lieutenant Howl drew his sword and slashed through the cords with a quick thrust.

"Whoa, be careful," Ethan said, jumping back. "You could have cut off our hands."

"Bilge water! That be foolish talk," the parrot squawked. "I be the best swordsman on the Seven Seas, and wouldn't cut a hair from yer head if I don't be meanin' to."

"Wow, your parrot can really talk," Dallin said walking around the lieutenant to get a better look at the large bird.

Putting his hand up to the parrot, he tried again,

"Polly wanna cracker?"

"I don't be knowin' no Polly, but ye can give me a cracker," the parrot said, bobbing his head up and down. "And while ye be at it, I wouldn't mind meetin' this here Polly, 'specially if she be a saucy parrot. A pirate life may be for me, but 'tis a lonely life. Squawk!"

Dallin laughed. "This is the coolest bird I've ever seen. What's his name Lieutenant?"

Lieutenant Howl looked at Dallin, but it was the parrot who answered. "The name be Lieutenant Howl, bucko." The lieutenant nodded.

"No, bird. Not the lieutenant's name, what's your name?" Ethan said, looking at the parrot.

"Blimey, fer magicians, ye ain't too bright," the parrot said, tilting his head sideways, and staring at the boys with one eye.

"What's that supposed to mean?" Ethan said.

"That means I be the brains of this here operation. Squawk!" the parrot answered with an extra loud squawk at the end for emphasis. Then he pooped on the lieutenant's shoulder for good measure, proving he was boss.

Thump...Thump...Thump...**Thump**

Hearing an ominous thumping sound getting closer, Ethan and Dallin turned to see a man with a wooden leg approach. He was a strange looking pirate. It was as if someone had taken a wilted cabbage, gave it eyes, Mr. Potato Head ears, and glued on a dinner roll

49

for a nose. He was the oldest, most wrinkled pirate onboard. Despite his apparent age and handicap, he had rippling muscles and a very hairy chest beneath his sleeveless vest.

Winking at the boys, the new arrival said, "What Lieutenant Howl be sayin' is that the parrot does the talkin'. Lieutenant here lost his tongue years ago, but somehow managed to train the bird to do his speakin' fer him."

"Cool," Dallin said. "So the parrot thinks he is Lieutenant Howl?"

"I don't *think* I be Lieutenant Howl, I *BE* Lieutenant Howl, savvy?" the parrot squawked with authority.

"Lieutenant 'Howl' sure is a funny name for a parrot," Dallin said.

"Yeah, he should change his name to Lieutenant 'Squawk'," Ethan suggested.

"Har, har, har," the peg-legged pirate laughed. "No one's ever thought of that before. I'll recommend it to the cap'n."

The lieutenant even smiled, though the parrot paced across his shoulders in silent protest.

"Who are you?" Dallin asked, staring at the man's wooden stump.

"I be Pegleg Kreg, the ship's gunner," he said. "I take care of the munitions, cannons and guns. What be yer names?"

"I'm Ethan, and this is my brother Dallin."

"How did you lose your leg, Mr. Pegleg?" Dallin asked.

"Dallin, it's not polite to ask stuff like that," Ethan interrupted, though he was just as curious as his brother.

"'Tis no matter, Master Ethan," Pegleg Kreg said. "I was on a pirate ship years ago. Back then Lieutenant Howl was part of the British Armada seekin' to capture us and end our piratin' ways. He finally caught up with us, and a sore battle ensued. Both our ships sank, and we drifted through shark-infested waters. By the time Cap'n Bartelmy came along and discovered us, only the lieutenant and meself were left."

"So did you lose your leg in the battle?" Dallin asked.

"Naw. As I was bein' pulled out of the water, one of the sharks decided he was still hungry."

"Everybody's got to eat," the parrot squawked matter-of-factly.

"Ever since then Lieutenant and me been part of Cap'n Bartelmy's crew. I never thought I'd be turnin' back to piracy, but here we are," Pegleg Kreg finished.

"Wow, what an adventure," Ethan said. "A chase across the sea, a pirate battle, shark-infested waters, and then saved just before being eaten. Your story would make a great book."

"Speaking of eating, I'm starving," Dallin exclaimed. "Have you got anything to eat?"

"Lunch ain't goin' to be ready for another hour or so," Pegleg said.

"What's there to do around here until lunch?" Ethan asked.

"Lots to do, lots to do," the bird said. "Swab the deck, trim the sails, mend the hatches, patch the leaks, repair the ropes…"

Interrupting Lieutenant Howl's list of chores, Pegleg said, "I came topside to train the crew 'bout bein' pirates. How would ye like to join us fer some trainin'?"

"Cool," Dallin said. "I always wanted to be a pirate."

Chapter 8
The Pirate Code

"All hands on deck. All hands on deck," the parrot squawked as Lieutenant Howl went to gather the men.

"Bosun," Pegleg Kreg called. "Help Lieutenant round up the crew for some pirate trainin', and tell 'em to bring their swords."

"Aye, aye." Yelling loudly he ordered, "All hands on deck! Bring yer cutlasses and move smartly mateys, or ye shall kiss the gunner's daughter!"

"Kiss the gunner's daughter?" Dallin wondered out loud. "Mr. Pegleg, are you going to let that mean pirate tell the crew they can kiss your daughter?"

"Har, har!" Pegleg laughed. "Nay, me daughter ain't onboard. What kissin' the gunner's daughter means is that they'll be punished with a whippin' if they don't hurry, savvy?"

"Man, pirates sure are mean," Ethan noted. "If we are late for class we just get detention or lines."

"Naw, we ain't never done it before. This here crew be a fair lot," Pegleg stated. "The bosun, he just likes soundin' tough. But now that I come to think 'bout it, kissin' me real daughter would be ripe punishment too. She looks just like me, poor lass, 'cept with more whiskers on her chin. I don't know which be worse, gettin' a whippin' or kissin' me daughter. Har, har, har."

The crew assembled on the deck, forming two lines opposite each other, cutlasses in hand. Many kept glancing at Dallin, fear in their eyes as if he were going to call the black plague down upon them.

"Hey Mr. Pegleg," Dallin said. "Can we have a sword and practice with the rest of the scallywags?"

"Aye, that's the spirit," Pegleg exclaimed with a crooked smile. "We'll make pirates out of ye yet. What say ye men? Shall we let the magicians have part in our fellowship?"

The silence on deck was thick enough to cut with a knife.

When no one dared answer, Captain Bartelmy looked down from the quarter deck and pronounced, "Only if they abide by the code."

"Aye," the crewmen agreed, nodding their heads repeatedly. "The code."

"What's the code?" Ethan asked.

"The code be the rules that we live and die by," Pegleg responded.

"Whoever heard of pirates having rules?" Dallin said. "I thought you just did whatever you wanted."

"Aye, but even amongst thieves there be honor," Captain Black Bart growled.

"Okay, so what are the rules?" Ethan asked.

"Rule number one," the captain called out from the helm. "Every man has equal vote in affairs of the moment, and equal title to grub and grog."

"What's grub and grog?" Dallin asked.

"Food and drink," Pegleg translated.

"Rule number two," the captain continued. "Ye must eat all yer vegetables."

"No way, that's one of my mom's rules too!" Dallin said.

"Ye don't want to be gettin' scurvy, now, do ya?" Pegleg said.

"Rule number three: never ask fer directions. Only rely on yer compass, the stars, a treasure map, or yer gut."

"Dad would make for a great pirate; he doesn't like to ask for directions either," Ethan mused.

"Rule number four: keep yer pistols and cutlass clean fer service. Rule number five: no fighting onboard; let every man's quarrel be ended on shore. Rule number six: candles out below deck by nine o'clock."

"That's my bedtime too," Dallin nodded.

"Rule number seven: the musician shall have rest on the Sabbath day, but the other six days and nights he works like the rest of us dogs."

"You have a musician?" Ethan asked. "I haven't heard any music except for your singing when we first got here."

"Alas, our musician followed rule number three and got lost when we laid anchor in the Caribbean a few months back. We ain't seen him since," the bosun lamented.

"Rule number eight: if an eye patch be needed, it must be black. No pink, yeller, purple or other girly colors. Rule number nine: no cryin' allowed, unless yer parrot dies, of course. Rule number ten: no hornswoggling another mate."

"What's horn-swoggle-ing?" Dallin asked.

"That means no cheatin' or stealin'," Pegleg again translated.

"Rule number eleven: durin' a swordfight, insults be required. Should neither man die, the pirate with the best insults be the winner. Lastly, rule number twelve…" Captain Black Bart paused for emphasis. "…no throwin' curses, hexes, or jinxes, and no voodoo, hoodoo, or doo-doo."

Raising his eyebrows in surprise, Dallin asked, "What's with the doo-doo?"

"We once had a shipmate bring a monkey onboard. Cunning little devil it was, throwin' doo-doo at everybody. We be so sick of monkey poop in our hair and food we marooned the little bugger on a deserted island," Pegleg grumbled, "And his master too."

"What's the punishment if we break any of the rules?" Ethan asked.

"The punishment fer breakin' the code…" Captain Black Bart declared, squinting at the boys, "Be the plank, maroonin', or dancin' with Jack Ketch."

"Dancing with another pirate doesn't sound that bad," Dallin said.

"You don't want to dance with Jack Ketch," Pegleg Kreg warned. "Jack Ketch be the hangman."

Dallin put his hands around his throat and gulped.

"That's okay, these are easy. We won't break the code. You should hear some of my mom's rules. Those are tough!" Ethan said. "Captain, we agree to honor the code. Can we be pirates now?"

Smiling for the first time, Captain Black Bart tipped his hat and said, "Give the magicians a sword me hearties, and let the trainin' begin."

"Aarrgh!" the crew yelled, raising their cutlasses in accord.

Chapter 9
A Pirate's Life for Me

"The first thing ye need to be learnin' men is how to look like a pirate," Pegleg Kreg announced, pacing between the two lines. "The carpenter has black paint down on the gun deck. After lunch, I want ye all to be gettin' a tattoo."

"Aarrgh," the pirates consented, and began chatting about the tattoos they would get. Things like flowers, a mermaid, rainbows, and even a fuzzy bunny were mentioned.

"I'm gonna get me a heart tattoo with me wife's name, Sissy, in the middle of it," a burly pirate announced.

Leaning over to his brother, Dallin sniggered, "These pirates are going to be laughed at, not feared."

"I was thinking the same thing," Ethan smirked. Waving his sword, he called out, "Uh, Mr. Pegleg, could you come here?"

"Yes, Master Ethan? Do ye be wantin' a tattoo?"

"No, thank you, my mom wouldn't approve," he said. "Dallin and I just thought you might be going about this the wrong way."

"What do ye mean?"

"I don't think people will be afraid of your crew if they have a bunch of tattoos with rainbows and fuzzy bunnies," Ethan said. "Those are not very scary."

"Shiver me timber, ye be right," Pegleg said in surprise. "Belay those ideas 'bout yer tattoos, mateys. New orders: fer now on there be no mermaids, butterflies, rainbows or the like. Approved pirate tattoos be skulls, daggers, ship's anchor, treasure chests and so on. Any questions?"

The burly pirate who wanted a heart with the name "Sissy" on it raised his sword.

"Yes, Mr. Mugwort?"

"Me wife won't be happy with me gettin' a tattoo," Mr. Mugwort admitted. "But if her name be on it, she might not get so mad."

"Aarrgh," several other pirates growled in agreement.

"What do ye think, Master Ethan?" Pegleg asked.

61

"That should be okay," Ethan yielded. "But only if her name is tattooed on a sword or other piratey stuff. No hearts and flowers."

"Aye, aye," the men agreed.

Thinking of what needed to be done next, a big goofy smile from one of the pirates caught Pegleg's attention

"Mr. Cuddle!" Pegleg growled at the short pirate. "Why are ye smilin'?"

"Uh, I changed me name to Darren Deeds, sir," Mr. Deeds corrected. "And I be smilin' 'cause I love bein' a pirate."

"Well smilin' ain't proper pirate protocol," Pegleg announced. "Pirates don't smile; pirates frown, pirates growl, pirates snarl and slobber."

Pacing between the men, he checked to make sure no one else was smiling. Dallin quickly wiped the grin off his face as Pegleg limped past.

"I see ye all need to be learnin' pirate manners, so let's start with yer growlin'," Pegleg decided. "Everyone hold up yer cutlass, bite the edge of the blade, like this, and give me yer best growl."

Ethan and Dallin bit the unsharpened side of their swords and growled with everyone else.

"Aarrgh!"

"Do ye call that growlin'?" Pegleg yelled. "Me grandma growls louder than that when she plucks her nose hairs. Ye need to growl like ye mean it, and put some slobber into it!"

Everyone growled again, spit flying.

"AARRRRGH!"

"Did I say purr like a kitten?" Pegleg yelled again. "No! I said growl like a dog, a dog that got its bone stolen! Growl like a lion that be gettin' its tail stepped on!"

"AARRRRRGH!"

Pegleg thumped down the line, nodding his approval. "Now remember mateys, when ye growl, show some teeth. If ye don't have many teeth, next time we be in port, melt down some gold coins and make yerselves some. If ye don't have any gold coins, I believe the cap'n knows a man who calls himself Mr. Den Teest, or somethin' ruther, and he'll knock 'em all out for free and give ye a new pair of wooden teeth."

Captain Black Bart nodded.

"Enough with manners fer today," Pegleg said. "Now, let's see some sword fightin'. I want ye all to pair off and practice."

After watching the pirates pair off and fight for a few minutes, Ethan and Dallin tried unsuccessfully to imitate their actions.

"No, no, no!" Pegleg said, hobbling over to the boys. "Ye ain't ever goin' to learn like that. Master Dallin, ye be about the same size as Mr. Cuddle, er, I mean Mr. Deeds, why don't ye two practice together. Master Ethan, ye match up with Mr. Killjoy."

Approaching the bald pirate, Ethan noticed something different. "When did you get an eye patch, Mr. Killjoy? You didn't have one earlier today."

"Me wife made it fer me, but she used some leftover cloth from her pink dress," Mr. Killjoy said, blushing. "I wasn't wearin' it yet 'cause I had to paint it black and wait fer it to dry. Do ye think it makes me look more piratey?"

"Uh, yeah, sure," Ethan stammered.

Lifting up the patch, Mr. Killjoy confessed, "Only problem is I don't be seein' too well with it over me eye."

Beneath the patch, the pirate had a black ring around his eye from the paint.

"Well, should we practice?" Ethan said, trying to change the subject without laughing at the big man.

Dallin was already underway with his training. He swung ferociously at Mr. Deeds, who blocked every thrust Dallin made.

"Good effort," Mr. Deeds complimented. "Ye have lots of energy, lad, but sword fightin' ain't just about attackin'. Those who attack the hardest don't always win. Ye need to defend yerself until an opportunity to strike opens up. As me pappy always said, 'The best offense be a good defense.'"

"Uh, okay," Dallin said, not really sure what Mr. Deeds meant.

"Let's take a break and watch yer brother," the short pirate suggested.

They watched as Ethan and Mr. Killjoy practiced swings and blocks in slow motion. Dallin was too impatient for this kind of training; he wanted to jump right in and swing away.

As Pegleg hobbled by, Dallin said, "Hey, aren't we forgetting something?"

"What do ye mean, Master Dallin?"

"It's too quiet. Aren't we forgetting about rule number eleven?" Dallin asked. "I thought sword fighting was supposed to include name-calling."

"Right ye be," Pegleg said. "Let's hear some insults, mateys."

Taunts and jeers filled the salty air as insults hurled across the deck like flying cannonballs. Names like "yeller-bellied scallywag," "pox-faced swabby," "son of a sea witch," "parrot-brained cabin boy" (which Lieutenant Howl's parrot took offense to), and "scurvy swine" were used as frequently as the pirates' cutlasses.

"Aarrgh, now this be the life for me, ye bilge rat," Dallin laughed, pulling out his short sword and attacking Darren Deeds again.

"That be the spirit! Now show me yer best pirate defense, ye hairless baboon," Mr. Deeds countered, spinning around Dallin and attacking from behind.

Dallin backed away as Mr. Deeds advanced with a daring sweep of his cutlass. Dallin put all his energy into his sword, and fought back heroically. As the two battled back and forth, the other pirates stopped fighting and watched, hooting and hollering for whomever they wanted to see win. Dallin's arm began to tire, and he was ready to give up when—

BEEP—BEEP

"Aarrgh," Mr. Deeds cried, dropping his cutlass and diving headfirst down an open hatch. All the other pirates followed his example and ran for cover.

Crouching in fear behind the wheel of the ship, Captain Black Bart peeked over the top. Ethan and Dallin were the only ones left standing on the deck. The rest of the crew were either hiding behind the mast, had climbed the ship's rigging, or run to the poop deck for safety.

"Uh-oh," Ethan mumbled.

"Ru—rule number twelve," the captain said hesitantly. "Ye promised ye wouldn't be doin' no voodoo or hoodoo."

Looking at his watch, Dallin said, "But Captain, I wasn't doing any voodoo or hoodoo. My watch won't hurt anyone; the beeping just means that it's lunch time."

As if on cue, the galley door swung open and Tough Cooky poked his head out. "COME AND GET IT! Grub be ready!"

"Oooh," the pirates murmured in astonishment as they climbed out of their hiding places and stared at Dallin. They all heard the magic beep, Dallin said it was lunchtime, and instantly his prophecy was fulfilled. Indeed, the young boy was a mighty wizard.

Chapter 10
Salmagundi

Dark splotches stained the table in the captain's quarters. Ethan and Dallin sat on hard wooden chairs, waiting for lunch to arrive. Their pirate training was fun, but they had worked up an appetite and were ready to eat. A young, scrawny cabin boy, not much older than Ethan, filled cups from a squat, long-necked bottle. Amber liquid spilled onto the table as the ship rocked from side to side, but no one seemed to notice.

Around the table sat Captain Black Bart, Lieutenant Howl with his parrot, and Dr. Freibeuter, the ship's doctor. When first introduced, he told the boys his name was pronounced "free-booter."

One of the helmsmen was steering the ship back to shore. They were moving fast; a storm out at sea was pushing the wind and waves toward the bay. At this rate, they would be safe on land before nightfall.

"These pirates could sure use some sippy-cups," Dallin said, noticing the spills on the table. "I bet their moms are not happy about all these stains."

"I bet you're right," Ethan laughed. The pirates sitting around the table just stared at them.

While waiting for lunch, Ethan and Dallin explained how they traveled through the treasure chest. They had to explain twice how they were born in America over three hundred years later, and that somehow when they climbed into the treasure chest back home it opened a doorway to the captain's treasure chest here.

Being a superstitious lot, and having already witnessed the power of Dallin's wristwatch and his uncanny ability to foresee the future, the pirates believed the story.

"Can I offer ye some rum, sirs," the cabin boy said with as much grace as possible.

"What's rum?" Dallin asked.

"Rum 'tis the captain's drink of choice," he answered. "Or would ye prefer whiskey."

"Whiskey?" Dallin said surprised. "Do you have root beer?"

"Sorry sir, no beer. Ale, perhaps?"

"What about lemonade?"

Seeing the blank looks on all the pirates' faces, Ethan asked, "Do you have water?"

"Aye," the junior pirate grunted.

"Water then, please," Ethan said.

"Water it be for all of us," the captain ordered reluctantly.

"Aye, aye, Cap'n," the boy said, bowing out of the captain's quarters.

Dallin watched the cabin boy retreat, and then turned around to admire the pirates sitting at the table. He was as happy as a kid on Christmas morning. He loved playing pirates; just as long as he never saw another plank again.

Ethan, however, was reminded of their predicament by the presence of the treasure chest sitting in the middle of the room. The captain had locked the latch since they last saw the trunk.

How are we going to get out of here, he thought. *The chest has to be the answer.* Then he remembered something that had been bothering him since speaking with Tough Cooky in the brig.

"Captain," Ethan began, drawing the man's attention away from Dallin's wristwatch. "Why did you turn pirate all of a sudden?"

Captain Black Bart squirmed uncomfortably in his chair. He glanced around the table, opened his mouth, and was about to speak when the door opened. The cook walked in carrying a large platter of food in one arm and a jug of water swinging from his left hook.

Putting down the food, Tough Cooky winked at the boys, filled their cups, then retreated with a bow.

"Ahh," the captain inhaled, breathing in the strong aroma. "Salmagundi."

"Gazoontite," Ethan said.

"Sprechen Sie Deutsch?" the doctor asked in German.

"Sorry, I didn't understand that. What did you say?"

"Do ye speak German?" Doctor Freibeuter asked, this time in English.

"No. Why do you ask?"

"You said 'gesundheit,' the German word for 'good health'." Doctor Freibeuter explained. "Why did you wish good health upon the captain?"

"I thought the captain sneezed. That's what we say when someone sneezes." Turning to the captain, Ethan asked, "What was it you said, Captain Black Bart?"

"Salmagundi, 'tis what we be havin' fer lunch," he answered, scooping food onto his plate and grabbing several hardtack biscuits. "Fish-Breath Cooky makes the best salmagundi." He didn't know the chef had changed his name to Tough Cooky.

Staring uneasily at the strange mix of stinky meat and vegetables on the platter, Dallin asked, "What exactly is sam-in-gun-di?"

"'Tis a delectable assortment of available meat and fish, Master Dallin," the doctor said in his refined accent. He was obviously better educated than the rest of the crew.

The doctor plopped a large scoop of it on Dallin's plate, and then another on Ethan's.

Dallin poked the bulging eyes of a fish head, then stabbed his fork into a piece of meat with an uncanny resemblance to a pig's foot. It smelled funny and looked slimy.

"I would prefer macaroni and cheese, or a peanut butter and jelly sandwich," Dallin mumbled.

"Come on, Dallin. What about your iron stomach?" Ethan teased.

"Let's see you take the first bite, then," Dallin said.

Ethan stuck his nose over his plate of glop and took a whiff. "No thanks, I'm not hungry," he said, pushing the plate back.

"Come now," Doctor Freibeuter said, "Ye two must be hungry after all thy pirate training."

"If ye wish, Master Ethan," the captain said, passing him a large jug with some yellowish-white pulpy sauce in it, "Try some of this special paste that I picked up from a German colony a few voyages back. It tones down the spice and adds somethin' special. I be puttin' this delicious pottage on everything I eat."

Afraid to say no, Ethan globbed a small scoop of the pulpy sauce onto a slimy chunk of meat and took a bite.

"Eww, sauerkraut!" Ethan declared, puckering his lips and scrunching up his nose.

The captain froze, his spoon hovering in front of his open mouth.

"What?" Ethan asked, chewing on the rubbery chunk of meat. "The salmagundi is not bad, but I don't like sauerkraut. My dad puts it on prime rib, but I can't stand the stuff."

Captain Black Bart's spoon clattered to the floor. His lower lip began to tremble, and then he burst into tears. He must have forgot rule number nine—no crying allowed—but Ethan wasn't about to remind him of that.

"Truly, ye be all-knowing magicians," he cried, tears rolling down his dirty cheeks. "How else would ye know what me wife called me?"

The tough captain, dressed all in black, with his mean scar, sank his head onto his arms and cried like a baby.

"I miss me wife," he sniffled. "But she thinks I be a stingy sour kraut."

Ethan got up, and though he swayed a little with the rocking of the boat, made his way over to the captain's side and patted him on the back.

"It's okay, sir. I miss my mom, too," Ethan consoled.

"How did ye know?" the captain asked, looking up at Ethan and wiping his soggy eyes. "How did ye know me wife called me a stingy sour kraut?"

"I thought she called you a stingy sour crust?" Dallin offered from across the table.

"No, no," the captain said, blowing his nose on his black sleeve. "'Tis right here, she calls me a stingy sour kraut."

The captain pulled out a crumpled piece of paper from his pocket and handed it to Ethan. It was a small piece of paper, apparently torn from a larger sheet. The note read:

Bartelmy:

Stingray, Sauer Kraut,
Take kids to Grandma's
house before Bartelmy gets
back, Burn Candles and

Ethan examined the piece of paper closely, with the lieutenant and doctor trying to see over his shoulder. This was the first time they had seen the note.

"Let me get this straight," Ethan began, smoothing out the paper on the table. "You arrived back from your voyage yesterday, went home, found your wife and kids gone, and this note sitting on the table, right?"

"Aye."

Ethan continued, "You read the note and thought she was calling you a stingy sour kraut, and that she was taking the kids and going back to her mother's house, leaving you all alone, right?"

"Aye," the captain grunted. "I don't be readin' too well, but it clearly says that Bartelmy be a stingy sour kraut. How could she call me a stingy sour kraut and take me kids away after eight wonderful years of marriage?"

"Captain Bart, I think I can help," Ethan said, his voice rising in excitement.

The captain perked up, his wet eyes full of hope. "Oh, if ye could help, Master Ethan, I would be willing to give ye anything, even all me treasure."

Chapter 11
Date Night

Ethan glanced over at Dallin and winked.

Dallin knew that when his brother winked, either he was going to try and pull a prank, or else he had a wonderful idea. Dallin hoped it was a wonderful idea. He was still a little worried that the captain might try to make them walk the plank again.

With a serious look on his face, Ethan said, "Okay Captain, I think my brother and I can save your marriage, but first you have to answer some questions."

"Anything, ask me anything at all," the captain said.

"Squawk! Ask away, ask away," the parrot said, getting excited.

"First, tell me Captain, what is your favorite thing to eat in the whole world?"

"Well, if I could be havin' anything me wants, I would be askin' fer a special fish dinner, the likes of which you would never believe, ye being a landlubber and all."

"Well, we are magicians," Ethan said, nodding to Dallin who was fiddling with his wristwatch. "Why don't you explain this tasty fish to me?"

"If ye say so," the captain said, eyeing Dallin suspiciously. "The most delicious fish is round and flat, as big as me table. It has a long, thin whip-like tail with a horn at the end of it that be as sharp as me dagger. Oh, and it swims through the ocean like a bird flies through the sky."

"Does anyone here know what this stinging ray-like fish is called?" Ethan hinted, glancing around the table at all three pirates.

The doctor and the lieutenant looked at each other and shrugged their shoulders.

"Bird-fish?" Lieutenant Howl's parrot squawked.

"The fishmongers at the market be callin' it a stingaree, me thinks," the captain said.

"We call it a stingray," Dallin said, poking at his salmagundi again.

Holding out the crumpled piece of paper to the captain, Ethan asked, "What does this word say right after your name, Captain?"

"Stingy," the captain answered, afraid to look at it.

"Are you sure?" Ethan prodded, holding the note directly in front of the captain's long nose.

Doctor Freibeuter and Lieutenant Howl leaned in for a peek.

The captain scratched his beard as he concentrated on his wife's flowing script. "This fancy writin' hurts me head."

"Just start with one letter at a time and try sounding it out, Captain," Ethan encouraged.

"Sttt—eeen—guh—rrr—aay," the captain sounded out. "Stingray!"

"By Jove, Captain, the young pup is a wizard!" the doctor exclaimed. "It doesn't say 'stingy,' it says 'stingray,' your favorite fish."

"Blow me down!" the parrot squawked.

"Shiver me timbers!" the captain exclaimed.

"That's what I be gettin' fer not payin' attention in me schoolin'. I should have done me homework, and practiced me cursive writing more. Thank ye, Master Ethan. I feel much better already."

Ethan beamed with pride.

Reading "stingray" from the note again, the captain's face darkened.

"But what about callin' me a sour kraut?" the captain said. "She still don't love me if she be thinkin' I be a sour kraut, and taking me daughters away."

His momentary excitement was fading quickly.

"Captain, what exactly do you think sour kraut is?" Ethan said.

"Uh, I don't really be knowin' exactly," the captain admitted. "But me thinks 'tis a mean person with a sour attitude?"

"Doctor Freibeuter, do you speak German?" Ethan asked.

"But of course," the doctor replied.

Holding up the pot that contained the yellowish-white pulp that the captain liked so much, Ethan asked, "What do Germans call shredded cabbage that ferments until it turns sour?"

The doctor thought for a moment. "I have not been in Germany since I was a young pup about your age, but I seem to remember a dish matching that description. I don't recall ever eating it, but I think it was called, uh, sour something...uh...Oh, I got it: sauerkraut."

"Stuff me with seaweed and call me a mermaid!" the captain cried, jumping out of his chair as realization dawned on him.

"Me beautiful wife was fixin' me most favorite dinner in the whole world and I up and left her," Captain Black Bart declared. "But what about me children goin' to me in-law's house?"

"That one's easy," Ethan said.

Turning to his brother, Ethan asked, "Dallin, when Mom and Dad want to go on a date, where do they send us?"

"To Grandma and Grandpa's house."

"I'm guessing that this note was a to-do list," Ethan said holding up the paper.

"What be a tu-du-liss?" the captain asked, raising his bushy eyebrows.

"A to-do list is a bunch of things that a person wants to get done. They write down what they need to do so they don't forget anything," Ethan answered. "I'm guessing your wife wanted to fix your favorite meal and was planning to drop the kids off at their grandma's house so she could have a nice, quiet evening alone with you."

Grabbing Ethan's hand and shaking it mightily, the captain cried for joy. "Ye be mighty wizards indeed. I'm going straight home and tell me wife how wonderful she be."

Kneeling in front of Ethan, Captain Black Bart removed a skeleton key from around his neck and handed it to him.

"Ye saved me from a terrible mistake, Master Ethan. Ye too, Master Dallin. Here be the key to me treasure chest. It be yours. From this day forward, let it be known that I be Captain Bartelmy, now and forever! The pirate, Captain Black Bart, is dead! Lieutenant, tell the bosun to lower the Jolly Roger. We be done with our piratin' ways."

"Aye, aye," the parrot squawked.

"Woo hoo!" Dallin yelled, running around the table and giving Captain Bartelmy a bear hug. "Can I throw the plank overboard, Captain?"

"I'll help ye do it, Master Dallin," the captain laughed. "I'll even give ye the Jolly Roger seein' how I won't be needin' the pirate flag no more."

"Cool," Dallin said.

"Dallin," Ethan said, holding up the skeleton key. "Forget about the plank. Let's go home."

"Ye mean back through the treasure chest?" Dr. Freibeuter asked.

Ethan nodded.

"Do ye have to go so soon?" the captain asked, with genuine sadness in his voice. Now that he was no longer the dreaded Captain Black Bart, he wasn't so scary. "We was just startin' to become friends."

"Can't we stay a little longer, Ethan?" Dallin asked. He was really enjoying himself, even though lunch wasn't very tasty. If he could just find some macaroni and cheese, everything would be perfect.

"I think we came for a reason," Ethan said. "We were supposed to help Captain Bartelmy. Now that we're done, we better get home before the magic wears off."

"Then go," the captain declared. "Me children, and their children's children shall honor the names of Master Ethan and Master Dallin forever."

The captain saluted the two boys, and the other men did the same. Even the parrot raised a wing in salute.

Ethan and Dallin ran to the chest. They were getting used to the swaying of the ship, and made it safely this time without crashing into anything.

Ethan inserted the skeleton key into the lock and turned.

The former pirates all watched with wide eyes.

CLICK, the latch popped open.

Turning to Captain Bartelmy, Doctor Freibeuter, and Lieutenant Howl and his parrot, Ethan smiled, waved goodbye, and then opened the lid.

Chapter 12
Stuck for Good

"Oh, no!" Ethan wailed.

Instead of an empty trunk, he saw a large pile of gold coins, rubies, emeralds and pearls. This was an amazing horde of treasure, but Ethan was very sad to see it again.

"Why is the treasure still here?" Ethan asked in surprise. He closed the lid and opened it again, hoping the gold would disappear.

"What's wrong?" Doctor Freibeuter asked.

"The treasure…" Ethan paused, thinking.

"Beauty, ain't she," Captain Bartelmy said, staring at the gold.

"…it should be gone," Dallin finished.

"Gone?" the doctor said. "That would be dark magic indeed."

"That is how we got here," Ethan said. "I don't think we can get back home with all the treasure still in the chest."

He stopped, staring at the captain and his men. Ethan was out of ideas.

"Well, then, let's dump it out," the captain suggested, walking over to the chest and grabbing a handle. "Someone help me."

The parrot flapped across the room and was the first one to the chest.

"Aarrgh, I'll help ye," the bird squawked landing on the opposite side. Lieutenant Howl followed behind.

Together, Lieutenant Howl and Captain Bartelmy tipped the chest over, spilling all the precious treasure onto the floor.

"There," the captain grunted, dropping the empty chest with a hallow thud. "See if it works for ye now."

"Thanks, Captain," Dallin said. "You know, you are not so scary when you're nice."

The captain grinned, his scarred eye as squinty as ever, but no longer intimidating.

Ethan opened the lid and climbed inside.

"Come on, Dallin, get in," Ethan said.

As Dallin climbed into the trunk next to Ethan, the doctor asked, "So what is going to happen after ye get inside?"

"When we close the lid and reopen the trunk, hopefully we will be back in our own house," Ethan said, kneeling down.

Crouching next to his brother, Dallin yelled, "Goodbye everybody. It was nice knowing you."

"Godspeed," the parrot squawked. "Next time don't be comin' without Polly. Squawk!"

The lid plopped shut.

Everything was quiet.

"Are we home yet?" Dallin whispered.

"I don't know. Let's open the lid and find out."

Slowly opening the lid, Ethan peeked out and was disappointed once again. They were still on the ship.

"So, did ye leave yet?" Doctor Freibeuter asked.

"Did ye bring Polly back with ye?" the parrot asked, hopping from one leg to the other.

"No, we never made it home," Ethan said sadly. "I think we are stuck here forever."

"Well now, 'tis not all that bad," Captain Bartelmy said. Excitement rising in his voice, he added, "I be havin' a grand idea. I promise that if ye can't get home, I'll take ye into me family. Ye can be like me own sons."

Ethan was still disappointed, but Dallin was catching the captain's excitement.

"Will you teach us more sword fighting and how to shoot guns and search for pirate treasure?" Dallin asked, jumping out of the chest.

Pulling out his cutlass, the captain swung his sword in the air and said, "I'll teach ye meself, and tell me wife that ye be me two new apprentices. Ye shall be the best sword fighters in the Seven Seas."

The captain pretended to fight with the lieutenant who pulled out his own cutlass and clashed blades with the captain.

"I'll skewer yer gizzard, ye lily-livered lizard," the parrot insulted as they parried blows back and forth, scattering gold coins and rubies across the floor.

"Woo hoo!" Dallin yelled, swinging his arm like the captain.

Ethan was not as excited. He closed the lid and sat down on top of the chest.

"Don't worry, lad," Doctor Freibeuter said. He sat next to Ethan and put an arm on his shoulder. "It will work itself out. Life isn't always fair, but I'm sure the magic will return when it is good and ready. Just be patient. Maybe there's still something left for thee and thy brother to do."

Looking up at the doctor, Ethan smiled. "Thank you, Doctor. Maybe you are right."

"Come and join us, Master Ethan," the captain beckoned while handing his cutlass to Dallin.

Getting off the chest, Ethan joined Dallin, taking the lieutenant's cutlass. For the rest of the trip back to shore, Captain Bartelmy and Lieutenant Howl—with the assistance of his parrot—continued to teach the boys the art of hand-to-hand combat, pirate style.

Chapter 13
The Witch

They made port before nightfall. As the brothers were rowed to shore in a longboat, Ethan glanced back, grateful to be off the ship. Painted on the stern in bold, black letters was a name: **Hades**.

That's a weird name for a boat, Ethan thought.

Reaching the dock, Captain Bartelmy helped Ethan and Dallin out of the longboat.

"Is it just me, or is the ground moving?" Dallin said, still swaying.

"Har, har," the captain laughed. "Now ye are startin' to get yer sea legs, Master Dallin."

Captain Bartelmy left the ship and crew in the care of Lieutenant Howl. Hailing a carriage, he and the boys, along with the treasure chest, headed for home.

"Won't the missus be surprised," Captain Bartelmy laughed as they rode up the cobblestone road. "She's always been wantin' boys, but we couldn't be havin' no more children after our two beautiful daughters."

In a serious tone he added, eyeing Dallin's wristwatch, "Just don't be doin' no magic if ye please. Me wife's mother be a witch, and it won't do no good for her to find out ye be magicians."

Ethan and Dallin exchanged looks.

"You know, we are not real magicians," Ethan said.

"Of course ye are," the captain said. "That medallion around Master Dallin's wrist is magic if I ever seen it."

Removing the watch and holding it out to the captain, Dallin said, "Back home everyone has one of these. It's called a digital watch."

Taking it between two fingers like it was going to bite him, the captain eyed it suspiciously. "What does it watch?"

Dallin laughed. "It doesn't watch anything. It is just called a watch."

"It's like a clock," Ethan explained. "It tells the time."

The watch beeped.

BEEP—BEEP

"Shiver me timbers," the captain yelled, dropping the watch like it was hot.

Laughing, Dallin picked it up.

"Sorry, it beeps for breakfast, lunch and dinner, my favorite times of the day. See, look here," Dallin said, pointing to the face of the watch. "It says the time is six o'clock right now: six, zero, zero. That's the time we eat dinner back home"

"Well, I'll be keelhauled!" the captain exclaimed. "But what about all that noise and the magic blue light?"

"That was just the alarm," Dallin said. "When you grabbed my wrist, you hit these two buttons on the side and made the alarm go off. Like this."

Dallin held in the two buttons for a few seconds. The alarm sounded, and the light flashed.

BEEP—BEEP—BEEP

Captain Bartelmy stared in amazement.

When the beeping and flashing stopped, Dallin handed it back to the captain.

"Here, you can have it," Dallin offered.

Taking the gift, the captain said, "That be mighty fine of ye."

Reaching into his long black jacket, the captain removed his two gold-handled daggers.

"Here," he said, handing one to each of the boys.

"I want ye each to have one of these."

"Cool," Dallin said, grabbing the knife by the handle.

"We can't take your daggers Captain Bartelmy," Ethan said, trying to hand it back. "These are yours, and they are probably very valuable."

"And I give them to ye," the captain said, smiling at the boys. "All the treasure ye saw in me chest I got by discoverin' an old pirate treasure map and diggin' it up, and then I almost became a pirate meself. Ye two lads saved me, so the treasure be yours. But I want ye to know, and never forget, there be more important things in life than pirate treasure."

Taking the dagger, Ethan said, "Okay, we'll take the daggers, but we don't want your treasure. Oh, I almost forgot."

Ethan removed the skeleton key from around his neck and handed it to the captain. "Here is your key back. I don't think we will need the chest until the magic returns, and I don't want to lose it."

The carriage rolled to a stop in front of a large stone house.

Climbing out of the carriage, the boys heard a squeal of delight from behind them.

Turning around, they saw two girls several years younger than themselves running out of the house. The girls sprinted to the captain and jumped into his outstretched arms.

"Aarrgh," the captain exclaimed, hoisting up his daughters. "Now here be me most valuable treasures in the whole world."

Throwing a pouch of coins to the carriage drivers, the captain said, "Bring in me trunk."

Carrying the giggling girls, the captain made his way into the house. Ethan and Dallin followed.

Entering the house, one of the captain's daughters called out, "Grandmamma, Papa's home!"

"You're late," an old woman's voice called out from the shadows.

Putting the girls down and removing his long jacket, Captain Bartelmy responded, "Hello to you too, mother-in-law. I didn't expect to be findin' ye here."

"Someone had to bring your daughters home. They were at my house last night, and I arrived here with them just minutes before you did. I was surprised to find that you were not home yet," she said, her old voice crackling.

"Yes, I had a tricky pirate encounter that needed dealin' with," the captain answered.

The girls "Ooo'ed" at the mention of pirates.

Captain Bartelmy winked at Ethan and Dallin. "Not to worry, these two lads helped sort out them nasty pirates before things got out of hand."

Moving aside, the captain continued, "Where are me manners? Let me introduce Master Ethan and Master Dallin, two aspiring sailors I be takin' on as me apprentices."

The girls curtsied. Ethan and Dallin bowed in return. When they glanced up, they saw the bent old woman smiling at them. Wispy gray hair framed a face full of wrinkles, a crooked nose, and a long chin that proudly displayed a large, hairy, black mole.

Both boys gasped.

"What's the matter, boys? You're not afraid of a little old witch, are you?" she cackled.

Before either could respond, the captain's wife ran into the room and threw her arms around her husband.

"Bart, you're home," she said with delight, squeezing the captain. "Come into the kitchen and take off your boots. The girls and I can't wait to hear about your adventures."

The captain allowed himself to be dragged into the kitchen by his wife and daughters, completely forgetting the two boys.

Ethan and Dallin looked at each other and then back at the old woman. She leaned on a twisted walking stick, staring at them intently.

"Are you the old woman who sold the chest to my father?" Ethan asked.

Before she could answer, the front doors opened and the carriage drivers barged in with the treasure chest.

"Bring that over here," she ordered, pointing to an empty spot on the ground in front of her.

They dropped the heavy trunk with a thump, and quickly retreated. They seemed afraid of the old woman. A minute later, Ethan and Dallin heard the clopping of horse hooves as the carriage pulled away.

"You did it, boys!" the old witch croaked. "My magic worked, and you figured it out. I must thank you for saving my daughter's family."

Chapter 14
The Traveling Trunk

"You *are* the old woman my dad saw!" Dallin exclaimed. "You're the one who sold him the magic chest!"

"Yes. Yes I am," the witch said. "I've been waiting hundreds of years for you two. Now I can finally rest in peace."

"What about us? How do we get home?" Ethan asked.

"The same way you got here," she answered. "Through the trunk."

"But it didn't work. We tried several times and the chest was always full of treasure," Ethan said.

"Yeah," Dallin agreed.

Sitting on the chest to rest her old bones, the woman beckoned the boys closer. "Lads, because of your quick wits and heroic actions, you have saved my son-in-law and helped him find his way back home. Without your assistance, Bartelmy would have become a dreaded pirate, and my granddaughters would have been without a father. Come, sit by me and I'll answer your questions as best I can."

Ethan and Dallin hesitantly walked over to the witch and sat in front of her.

"First, how did we get here?" Ethan asked.

"Through the traveling trunk," she answered.

"No, what I mean is, why did we come here?" Ethan said.

"My precious granddaughters needed help, so I made this magic trunk to bring help," the witch said. "I've waited hundreds of years for children with enough imagination to activate the traveling powers and come to the rescue."

"But, how did you know to choose us?" Dallin asked.

"I didn't choose you—you chose yourself," she said. "Over the years I have given the trunk to many children, but all have failed to use their imagination and unleash the magic. Many years I have waited, and many children have owned the trunk, but only you two opened the door."

"Cool," Dallin breathed.

"The power of the traveling trunk is now yours. It can open the door to any time and any place you can imagine. But beware, the magic will not work in the presence of adults. You may face danger, but if you use your imagination and wits, you will be safe, and have many wonderful adventures."

"How will we know when the traveling trunk is working?" Ethan asked.

Lifting her walking stick, the witch struck the lock on the treasure chest, breaking it off in a flash of bright blue light.

"The power of your imagination will activate the trunk and deliver whatever clothing is necessary for your next adventure. Put on the clothes, climb into the trunk, and the magic will take you wherever you are needed. When you are ready to go home—and there are no unimaginative adults present—your own clothes will reappear inside the trunk that you traveled through."

Going to the fireplace, the witch said, "Ethan and Dallin, your mission here is complete. Do you accept the power of the traveling trunk?"

"Absolutely!" Dallin exclaimed.

"Uh, sure," Ethan said, though not quite as enthusiastically.

"Thank you, lads. You may go home now." With that, the witch threw a handful of powder into the fireplace and disappeared in an explosion of light and thunder.

When the smoke cleared, and they could see again, the old woman was gone.

Everything was quiet except for the laughter coming from the kitchen. Captain Bartelmy and his family must not have heard the thunder, for no one came running into the room. Either that, or they were used to the old witch using her ka-boom powder whenever she left.

"Come on, Dallin, let's go home," Ethan said, grabbing his brother's arm. Walking over to the treasure chest, Ethan lifted the lid and was relieved at what he saw. "Yes! Our own clothes are in here."

They quickly removed their cabin-boy rags and put on their regular clothes and shoes.

Staring at the kitchen door, Dallin said, "Should we go say goodbye?"

"We can't," Ethan said sadly. "Remember, the witch said it wouldn't work if adults are around."

Glancing about the room one last time, they climbed into the chest and closed the lid.

Chapter 15
Treasure Map

When the boys opened the treasure chest lid, they were overjoyed to see familiar surroundings: the forest-painted walls, their bunk beds shaped like the branches of a massive tree, their giant LoveSac beanbag, and the black pirate flag, the Jolly Roger, lying on their bedroom floor.

"We're home!" Ethan yelled, jumping out of the trunk.

"Woo hoo!" Dallin cheered, climbing out behind Ethan.

They hopped up and down giving each other high-fives. They were so excited they didn't notice their sister standing in the open door.

"E-hen, Da-win, why you hiding?" Kaitlyn asked.

"Kaitlyn!" Dallin said. "Have you been standing outside our door the whole time we were gone?"

Without waiting for a response, Ethan said, "Come

on, Dallin, we need to tell Mom and Dad we're back. I bet they are worried sick that we've been gone so long."

Running from their room, they charged down the hallway to their parents' bedroom yelling, "Mom, Dad, we're back! We're okay! We made it back safely!"

Barging in, they saw their dad starting to lie down.

"What's all the yelling about?" Dad asked with a confused and tired expression on his face.

"We're back, Dad!" Dallin blurted out.

"Yeah, we've been gone all day," Ethan said. "The chest you gave us is magic! We climbed inside, and when we got out we were on Captain Bartelmy's pirate ship. We helped save him from becoming a bad pirate, Dad!"

"It was so cool," Dallin chimed in. "We almost walked the plank, but were saved by my wristwatch. So the pirates taught us how to swordfight, we ate salmagundi, and then met the old witch who sold you the trunk. She said we did a good job and gave us the magic of the traveling trunk."

"You boys sure come up with a story fast. I just left your room five minutes ago. Now, let me take a nap and then we can all play pirates, okay?"

Overhearing the conversation, their mom walked into the bedroom. "Now boys, you know Dad is tired. He needs a nap so we can go on our date tonight. And don't forget, you're going over to Grandma's house while we go out."

Ethan winked at Dallin.

"Go along and play with your new treasure chest," Mom said, shooing them out of the bedroom.

"The chest! Our toys! Our toys must be back," Dallin blurted out. "Quick, to the traveling trunk!"

Charging back up the hall, they almost knocked Kaitlyn over in their rush. When they reached the treasure chest they grabbed the lid, looked at each other, and then slowly lifted.

"Ah, man!" Dallin sighed, disappointed to see all his old toys again.

"At least everything is back to normal," Ethan said.

"Yeah, but we forgot our daggers. They were with the pirate clothes."

Staring down into the trunk, Dallin noticed something shiny underneath his baseball glove.

"Hey, what's that?" Dallin pointed.

"Our daggers!" Ethan exclaimed, pulling them out.

Tied to one of the daggers was an old piece of yellow parchment.

"What is it?"

"It looks like an old treasure map," Ethan said, unrolling the fragile paper.

"Check out the back—there's writing on it," Dallin observed.

Turning it over, Ethan and Dallin read:

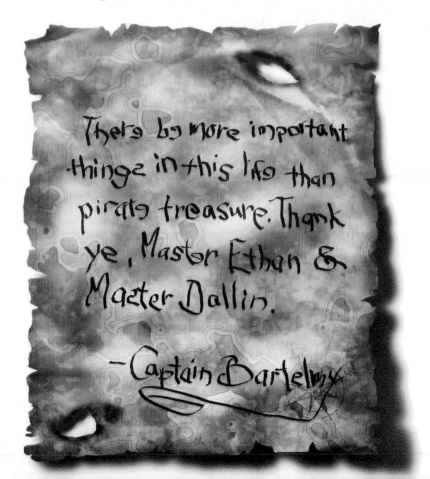

There by more important thinge in this life than pirate treasure. Thank ye, Master Ethan & Master Dallin.

—Captain Bartelmy

Dallin's Pirate Dictionary

(Corrections made by Ethan)

Ahoy : Pirate way of saying, "Hey man, what's up?"

All Hands on Deck : What you yell to get the entire crew up on deck fast. Heard most often after someone farts below deck.

Aarrgh!
who farted?

Aarrgh : What pirates say when they can't think of anything else to say, which means they say it a lot.

Accord : Like a rope, used to tie up your hand before walking the plank. (It means an agreement. If you have an accord with a pirate, then you have an agreement.)

Honk!

Black Spot : What is on a pirate's bandana after he blows his nose in it a few times. (A piece of paper with a black spot on it is given to a pirate as a warning that he is marked for death.

ooow!

Booty : What the captain kicks if someone isn't pulling their weight onboard.

(Pirate word for stolen treasure.)

Bow : The front of the ship. Pronounced bow, like a dog barking "bow-wow."

bow-wow!

Brig : Prison on a pirate ship.

Buccaneer : How much pirates pay for an ear of corn. (French word for Pirate, though it originally meant "barbeque." Maybe the first Caribbean pirates liked to eat a lot of BBQ.)

Cap'n : A short Captain. (No, not a short Captain; just a short way to say "Captain.")

Caribbean : I think cocoa is made from carob beans, so the Caribbean must be where cocoa is produced. (Islands located in the Caribbean Sea between Florida and South America.)

Chest : Pirates like to show off their hairy chests by not wearing a shirt under their vest.

(A trunk where pirates store their booty.)

do ye like me chest?

Arrgh! Move over birdbrain!

Crow's Nest : Where crows sleep at night. But since crows are lousy talkers, pirates soon turned to parrots instead. (A lookout point at the top of the highest mast of a ship, and a great place to drop water balloons from.)

Cutlass : What pirates tell the barber if they want to keep their beards long. (A curved pirate sword.)

Cutthroat : What happens to pirates who don't follow the captain's orders.

(This is what the really mean pirates were called. You can still find cutthroats today, but they normally wear suits and work at the top of skyscrapers.)

Davy Jones' Locker : Where the young Davy Jones kept his school books.

He also kept his swords, treasure maps, and other pirate stuff hidden in his locker so the school principal wouldn't find them. (The imaginary place at the bottom of the ocean where Davy Jones waits to escort dead pirates to the other side.)

Deck : To punch someone, probably because they blew their nose on your bandana and gave it a nasty black spot. (The top floor of a ship, which by the way, is where most of the punching takes place.)

What ye be sayin' bout me Mum?

Galley : The place where the cook invents the most horrible foods imaginable to torture crewmates with.

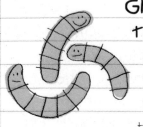

Grub : Short, fat worms that turn into beetles. My dad tried to get me to eat one once. (Pirate word for food; and yes, our dad did try to get us to eat a grub once; a big, fat, juicy one.)

yeeeowww!

tee hee

Hardtack : Short pokey things that naughty kids put on the seat of their teacher's chair. (Stale biscuits, and the closest thing to bread that pirates ever get onboard.)

Haven : Where good people go when they die. (That's heaven, Dallin. Haven is a safe place for pirates to hang out, party, and recruit new members.)

Helm : A big wooden wheel the captain turns to steer the ship.

Hull : Where pirates bury their treasure chests; the deeper, the better. (Pirates bury their treasure in a hole, not hull. The body of a ship.)

Jolly Roger : The nice name pirates give to their black flag with the skull and crossbones. Pirates must love the name Roger.

arrrgh! me be next!

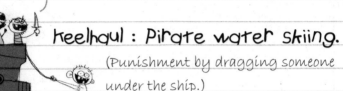

keelhaul : Pirate water skiing.

(Punishment by dragging someone under the ship.)

pucker up, lover boy!

kiss the Gunner's Daughter : Eww, kissing girls is gross! (Punishment by flogging or beating with a whip while the victim lies on top of a cannon like he is kissing it.)

Landlubber : Someone who has never been on a boat.

Maroon : Either a coconut cookie, or the color purple, but I'm not sure what it has to do with pirates. (Leaving someone to die on a deserted island with little or no food and water. This form of punishment made pirates feel less guilty because the unlucky person would not actually be killed by his former friends.)

Mast : Catholic church services on Sunday. (A tall pole in the middle of a ship that the sails and ropes are attached to.)

Matey: What you call your pirate friends.

Mutiny : A short pirate who can't speak; mute and tiny. (When the crew maroons the captain and elects a new leader. Mutiny probably happened in many cases because the captain didn't give his pirates a good dental plan, which would explain all the missing teeth.)

parlay

salmagundi
yucky

Parlay : The bushy green stuff you get on your plate at fancy restaurants.

(That's parsley. Parlay means to negotiate.)

Peg Leg : The name given to any pirate who has lost a leg to cannibals or while swimming in shark-infested waters.

shark got me leg

har har

Poop Deck : Where the toilets are on a pirate ship. (The poop deck is the highest deck at the back of the ship above the captain's quarters. If anyone tried to poop on the poop deck, they would probably be marooned at the next deserted island.)

Prow : What animals do when hunting for food. (That is prowl, Dallin. Prow is the front, pointy end of the ship.)

Salmagundi : Gross pirate food. If you ever see this on the menu, go to a different restaurant.

Savvy : I don't know what it means, but pirates like to say it. (The pirate way of saying, "Get the picture?")

Aaahhhh!

Shark Bait : What pirates call prisoners who are going to walk the plank.

Spyglass : Telescope, most often used to look for booty.

Starboard : When pirates get bored of watching reruns on TV.

yo, ho, ho hum

(The right side of the ship when facing the pointy end. Pirates didn't have TV.)

Stern : A mean pirate. (Actually, the stern is the back of the ship. But since most captains had mean attitudes, and they could always be found at the back of the ship, pirates began calling other people with mean attitudes "stern.")

Weigh Anchor : To see how much an anchor weighs, though who really cares? (It doesn't mean to weigh it. It means to raise the anchor out of the water so the ship can sail away.)

I reckon I be not enjoyin' this here job

yo-Ho-Ho : What Santa Claus said back in the days of pirates. All pirates loved Santa because it was a chance to get free booty. But since they were always naughty, Santa never came. (I never heard any pirates say this, but it seems like a very piratey thing to say.)

free booty, me eye, arrgh!

booty

1) Mail Away request must be postmarked within 30 days of purchase.

2) Fill-in and cut out this Mail-Away Form in it's entirety.

3) Send a photocopy of the book's UPC code.

4) Make check or money order of **$5.00** for Shipping and Handling payable to Flinders Press.

5) Mail in: **1.** Completed mail-away form; **2.** Copy of UPC code found on the back cover; **3. $5.00** S&H check or money order, to:

Flinders Press, Inc.
Pirate Flag Promo
P.O. Box 3975
Burbank, CA 91508-3975

3 Feet

5 Feet

Cut along dotted line and mail in below potion with UPC code and S&H payment.

Customer Information   MAIL-AWAY FORM

Please print clearly

Name:_____

Purchase Date_____ Where Purchased_____

Address:_____ City_____
(No P.O. Boxes)

State_____ Zip_____ Phone_____

Email_____ Required Signature_____

☐ No, do not email promotional information about future Traveling Trunk Adventure Books.

Available in USA Only

1) Your book receipt or invoice must have a date of purchase between January 2010 - December 2010. Qualifying book is any of the *Traveling Trunk Adventure* series. 2) Offer applicable to participants within the United States of America only. 3) Offer rights cannot be transferred. 4) Offer void where prohibited, taxed or restricted by law. 5) Completed Mail-Away form, copy of UPC, and payment for Shipping and Handling (S&H) must be received together by Flinders Press postmarked within 30 days of purchase. Photocopies are acceptable. Keep copies of all items mailed. 6) ***End Users ONLY***. Only one offer per household. Requests from groups, P.O. Boxes, organizations, or resellers will not be honored. Dealers, distributors and other resellers are not eligible for this offer. 7) This offer is only available while supplies last. 8) Proof of mailing does not constitute proof of delivery. Flinders Press is not responsible for lost, late, illegible, misdirected or postage due mail. Any request postmarked or received after applicable dates will be returned as ineligible. 9) If terms and conditions are not met, rebate claim will be rejected without notice. Incomplete or illegible submissions will not be returned, and check or money order will be destroyed. 10) Bounced or returned checks for any reason will be disqualified without notice. 11) Allow 8-12 weeks, after receipt of Mail-Away form and complete documentation, for processing. Design, style and exact size of flags may vary. Flag is approximately five feet wide by three feet high. 12) This offer is subject to change or cancellation at any time without notice.

Cut along dotted line and mail in below potion with UPC code and S&H payment.

Traveling Trunk Promo: Free Pirate Flag

Flinders Press, Inc.
Pirate Flag Promo
P.O. Box 3975
Burbank, CA 91508-3975

www.flinderspress.com